Parents and Caregivers,

Stone Arch Readers are designed to provide enjoyable reading experiences, as well as opportunities to develop vocabulary, literacy skills, and comprehension. Here are a few ways to support your beginning reader:

- Talk with your child about the ideas addressed in the story.

- Discuss each illustration, mentioning the characters, where they are, and what they are doing.

- Read with expression, pointing to each word. You may want to read the whole story through and then revisit parts of the story to ensure that the meanings of words or phrases are understood.

- Talk about why the character did what he or she did and what your child would do in that situation.

- Help your child connect with characters and events in the story.

Remember, reading with your child should be fun, not forced. Each moment spent reading with your child is a priceless investment in his or her literacy life.

Gail Saunders-Smith, Ph.D.

STONE ARCH READERS

are published by Stone Arch Books, a Capstone Imprint
1710 Roe Crest Drive
North Mankato, Minnesota 56003
www.capstonepub.com

Library of Congress Cataloging-in-Publication Data
Klein, Adria F. (Adria Fay), 1947-
Circus Train / by Adria Klein ; illustrated by Craig Cameron.
p. cm. -- (Stone Arch readers: Train time)
Summary: Circus Train pulls in to town, and each kind of
animal is in it's own brightly colored car.
ISBN 978-1-4342-4188-7 (library binding)
ISBN 978-1-4342-4883-1 (pbk.)
1. Circus trains--Juvenile fiction. 2. Circus animals--Juvenile
fiction. 3. Colors--Juvenile fiction. [1. Circus trains--Fiction.
2. Trains--Fiction. 3. Circus animals--Fiction. 4. Animals--Fiction.
5. Color--Fiction.] I. Cameron, Craig, ill. II. Title.
PZ7.K678324Cir 2013
[E]--dc23
2012026288

Reading Consultants:
Gail Saunders-Smith, Ph.D.
Melinda Melton Crow, M.Ed.
Laurie K. Holland, Media Specialist
Designer: Russell Griesmer

Printed in the United States of America in North Mankato, Minnesota.
062017   010565R

Circus
Train

written by
Adria F. Klein

illustrated by
Craig Cameron

STONE ARCH BOOKS
a capstone imprint

The Circus Train was in town.

Toot! Toot!

"Here I am!" he said.

Look at all the animals!

There were lions in the
yellow car.

There were tigers in the
orange car.

There were bears in the
brown car.

There were elephants in the
gray car.

There were monkeys in the
red car.

There were dogs in the
white car.

There were horses in the
black car.

Who is in the last car?

The clowns!

"Time for fun!"
said Circus Train.

STORY WORDS

circus   town   clowns

train   animals

Word Count: 81